Estelle's Reward

Adapted from a Guernsey folktale

by Wendy Body

LONGMAN

On a misty-soft island morning when the early sun played with the dew on the grass, Estelle walked across the fields to her home. She was tired, for she had spent the long night nursing a friend's sick child. As the day had broken, so had the little girl's fever – allowing Estelle to leave the sleeping child to the care of her mother.

People said Estelle had a gift for looking after the sick and the troubled, and they often came to seek her help. Her kindly face had seen many a problem and her cool hands had comforted many an ailing child.

Now, however, as she sighted her cottage across the final field, all that was on her mind was a sleep in her comfortable old armchair.

But this was not to be.

From behind the large group of weathered old stones, which sprawled to one side of the field, appeared a man. Estelle did not recognise him as he walked towards her.

She watched his dark, glowing eyes and his pointed face as he began to speak. He told her that there was a sick baby who urgently needed her help and he pleaded with her to follow him. Tired as she was, Estelle agreed to see the child.

Back across the fields she followed the silent man. She was puzzled when it seemed that he was leading her to the coast, for she knew that there were no houses on that part of the shore. But something about the man prevented her asking questions.

Soon, accompanied by the sound of breaking waves and the mournful cry of seagulls, they reached the entrance to a cave. Estelle knew it to be a dark, damp and gloomy place and so was surprised when she saw a soft glow of light coming from inside.

As she went into the cave, Estelle drew an astonished breath.

Gone were the dark granite walls
she had seen before, gone were
the hidden pools and clusters of
slippery weed. Instead the walls
were sparkling in the soft
glowing light as if studded with

a thousand jewels. Smooth
golden sand spread out on
each side of a silvery path and
strange but beautiful flowers
waved gently as they brushed
against her skirt.

On they went into the cave until they reached a large heavy door. The man opened it and Estelle followed him as he went through one large room and into another. Both rooms were richly furnished and breath-taking to behold. In the centre of the second room stood a delicately made golden cradle. Estelle walked up to it and peered in. There lay a baby – a very sick baby as Estelle could tell from her first glance.

"Will you nurse the child?" the man asked.

In spite of the strangeness of the situation, Estelle knew that the child needed her help – and she could never refuse the needs of a sick child.

"I will," she replied.

"Whatever you need will be provided," the man said. "Simply ask."

And so it was. Anything Estelle
needed for the baby or for herself
was brought to her by a short,
dark-haired youth dressed in a
green tunic who bore a strong
resemblance to the baby. He
never spoke except to ask how
the child was.

The baby slowly improved with Estelle's skilled nursing and gradually he began to chuckle and gurgle in his cradle. He would gaze at her with huge green eyes. Sometimes it seemed as if he was amused by some secret. Occasionally, he would reach up and touch her face as she bent over to feed or change him.

While the baby was sleeping, Estelle often gazed at her surroundings and wondered at the strangeness of it all. Who were they – the man, the youth and the baby? Where was the baby's mother? They looked human but were they? It seemed to her that she was woven into the spell of some faery enchantment, but she decided it would be safer to say nothing about it to the man or the youth.

On the third morning, the baby
seemed to have recovered
completely. Estelle changed and
fed him and then began to play
with him.

She tickled him under the arms and the baby gurgled with pleasure. She held him high in the air above her head and he chortled and chuckled. As he looked down into her face, dribbling and laughing, some of the baby's dribble fell into Estelle's eye.

She put him back into the cradle and wiped her face.

Estelle lowered her handkerchief and opened her eyes. The splendours of the room had vanished. Gone were the sparkling walls and rich furnishings and gone was the golden cradle.

Around her were the damp walls
of the cave and underfoot were
pebbles, damp sand and seaweed.
The baby was lying on a rock
watching her... smiling.

At that moment, the man appeared from the end of the cave where the door had been. Estelle decided it was safer to say nothing about what had happened. The man might be angered if he realised that his faery enchantment had been broken.

So she looked steadily at the man and said, "The child is well again and no longer needs my care. May I return to my own home?"

"Certainly," the man replied. "That is what I came to tell you. I am grateful to you for saving the child's life and I wish to repay you."

With that, he handed Estelle a small leather pouch. She heard the clink of money as she grasped it. Opening the bag, Estelle was astonished to see that it was filled with golden coins.

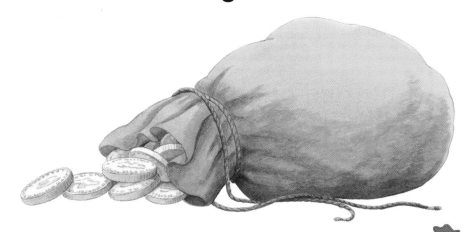

"Thank you, sir," she said, breathlessly, putting the pouch into her pocket. "Now I shall be on my way."

Estelle bent over the baby and touched his cheek as she said goodbye. The baby's eyes glittered and sparkled and he seemed to be laughing at the secret they shared. The man watched Estelle as she turned and left.

She hurried out of the cave, looking back once or twice to see if she was being followed.

Out on the beach, she closed her eyes for a moment against the bright light of the early morning sun. She breathed deeply and the cool salty air filled her lungs.

On the way home she stopped to gather some fresh plump mushrooms in her shawl for breakfast. When she reached her cottage, a woman was waiting. Estelle recognised her as the grandmother of the little girl who she had recently nursed.

"Estelle, I wanted to thank you for nursing my granddaughter all last night," said the woman. "I was surprised to get here before you, but I see that you stopped to gather mushrooms on your way home."

"I was glad to help," murmured the weary Estelle as she bade farewell to the woman and went into the cottage.

"Last night?! What did she mean?" Estelle asked herself. "I must have misunderstood her."

She hid the gold coins safely away in the dresser – grateful for the security they would offer in the years to come.

Three days later, Estelle was in the market shopping for food. As she browsed among the stalls, she suddenly spotted the dark-haired youth in his green tunic. He was stealing the choicest fruits and vegetables – invisible to all but Estelle.

"Stop!" Estelle cried, catching hold of the youth's arm. "I see what you are doing!"

The faery youth stared darkly into her eyes for a long moment before he spoke: "You see me, do you? Well, you shall also see that what one faery can give, another faery can take!"

With that, he wrenched his arm from Estelle's grasp and escaped.

"What one faery can give, another faery can take..." Estelle repeated to herself. Then she realised what the youth meant.

She gathered up her skirts and ran swiftly back to the cottage. Would the gold still be hidden in the dresser?

Estelle pulled the leather pouch from its hiding place. The coins were still there but even as she saw and felt their cold comfort, the gold disappeared and she was left with only a handful of pebbles.

Estelle sighed a moment of regret and then she smiled.

She had saved the baby's life, perhaps that was reward enough....